W9-CBX-455

CHRISTOPHER FORD
STICKMAN ODYSSEY
BOOK TWO: THE WRATH OF ZOZIMOS
SLAM
PHILOMEL BOOKS
An Imprint of Penguin Group (USA) Inc.

PHILOMEL BOOKS
A division of Penguin Young Readers Group.
Published by The Penguin Group. Penguin Group (USA) Inc., 375 Hudson Street, New York, NY 10014, U.S.A. Penguin Group (Canada), 90 Eglinton Avenue East, Suite 700, Toronto, Ontario M4P 2Y3, Canada (a division of Pearson Penguin Canada Inc.). Penguin Books Ltd, 80 Strand, London WC2R 0RL, England. Penguin Ireland, 25 St. Stephen's Green, Dublin 2, Ireland (a division of Penguin Books Ltd). Penguin Group (Australia), 250 Camberwell Road, Camberwell, Victoria 3124, Australia (a division of Pearson Australia Group Pty Ltd). Penguin Books India Pvt Ltd, 11 Community Centre, Panchsheel Park, New Delhi – 110 017, India. Penguin Group (NZ), 67 Apollo Drive, Rosedale, Auckland 0632, New Zealand (a division of Pearson New Zealand Ltd). Penguin Books (South Africa) (Pty) Ltd, 24 Sturdee Avenue, Rosebank, Johannesburg 2196, South Africa.
Penguin Books Ltd, Registered Offices: 80 Strand, London WC2R 0RL, England.

Published simultaneously in Canada.
Printed in the United States of America.

Edited by Michael Green.
Design by Richard Amari.

The doodles and stick figures in this book were rendered with a Wacom Cintiq 21UX.

Library of Congress Cataloging-in-Publication Data
is available upon request.

ISBN 978-0-399-25427-7
1 3 5 7 9 10 8 6 4 2

For Tricia

AND NOW, A
STICKMAN ODYSSEY
BOOK ONE RECAP
WITH THE ONE-EYED WITCH
IF YOU'RE READING THIS VILE TOME, YOU PROBABLY WANT TO KNOW WHAT'S GOING ON WITH THAT ZOZIMOS GUY.
YEE HEE HEE!
WHAT A DUMMY! HE SPENT THE WHOLE LAST BOOK LOOKING FOR STICATHA AND HE HASN'T EVEN FOUND IT YET!
YOU SEE, HIS UNCLE NESTOR RAISED ZOZIMOS TO GET REVENGE ON THE WITCH WHO KILLED HIS FATHER AND STOLE HIS KINGDOM OF STICATHA.
NOT ME, ANOTHER WITCH.

LET'S SEE, WHAT ELSE SHOULD YOU KNOW?
OH! ZOZIMOS' SWORD HAS A PROPHECY FROM SOME GHOSTS, SO YOU KNOW IT'S GONNA COME TRUE!
THE PROPHECY SAYS ZOZIMOS WILL SLAY ASTERIA HERE WITH HIS FATHER'S SWORD.
THAT'S PRETTY MESSED UP. EVEN FOR ME.
WELL, THAT'S IT. GO AHEAD AND READ THE BOOK IF YOU STILL WANT TO. WASTE OF TIME, IF YOU ASK ME.
DOESN'T ANYONE WANT TO KNOW MY STORY ABOUT MY MISSING EYEBALL?
?

EDGE OF THE WORLD
TELETOPIA
WEST WIND
GREAT WHIRLPOOL
MARINOS
CANDY ISLAND
ODONOROS
NAUTICA
ARCHAEA
STAR
FALLEN COL

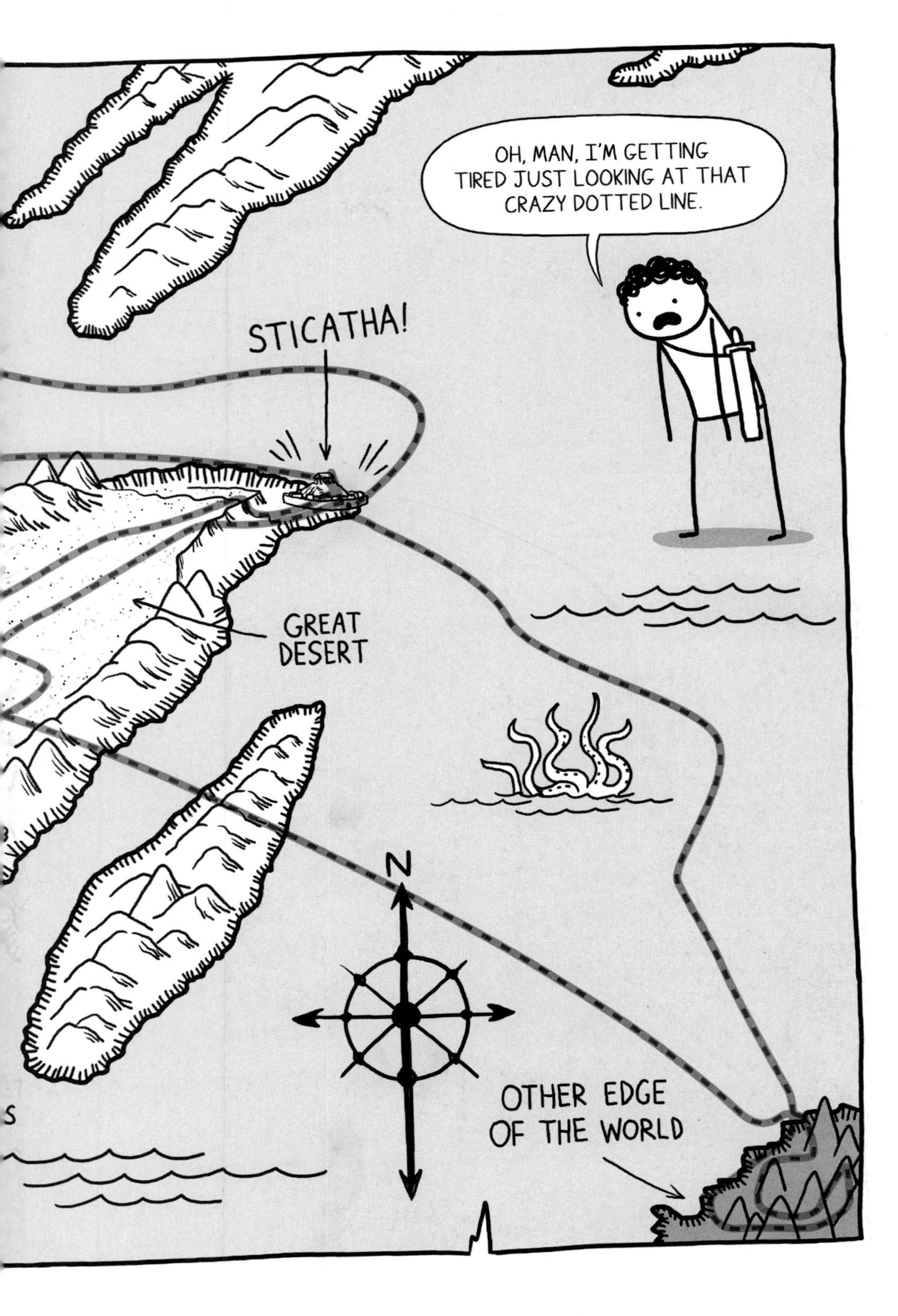
OH, MAN, I'M GETTING TIRED JUST LOOKING AT THAT CRAZY DOTTED LINE.
STICATHA!
GREAT DESERT
N
OTHER EDGE OF THE WORLD

PART ONE

SING, O MUSE, OF THE WRATH OF ZENON'S SON -- FAR-WANDERING ZOZIMOS.
MMMPH!!
SING HOW HIS WRATH LED HIM INTO TROUBLE AGAIN AND AGAIN...
MBRLXSK!
...LIKE WHAT HE'S DOING RIGHT HERE.
ZOZIMOS!
FWIP!

DONK!
WATCH IT, CLUMSY.
MMMPH!!
GOT SOMETHING TO SAY FOR YOURSELF?
UNTIE
UNTIE
WOULD YOU UNTIE ME?! I TOLD YOU -- I'M NOT GOING TO STICATHA UNTIL I HELP MY FRIENDS!
LET'S CAMP IN THIS GROVE TONIGHT.

EAT SOMETHING. YOU'RE SKIN AND BONES!
I CAN'T EAT, TIED UP LIKE A PRIZE GOAT!
GET USED TO IT. GONNA BE A LONG RIDE TO STICATHA, ZOZIMOS.
RUSTLE
?
WHAT KIND OF UNCLE ARE YOU? I WAS GOING TO GO TO STICATHA EVENTUALLY!
GO ON, EAT UP, WHINY-PANTS.

YOU'VE BEEN DILLYDALLYING!!
WHAT IS THAT SUPPOSED TO MEAN?!
WANDERING, LOLLYGAGGING, TIME-WASTING! WHAT HAPPENED TO YOUR QUEST TO RECLAIM STICATHA?
I SWORE AN OATH TO HELP MY FRIENDS FIRST.
I DIDN'T RAISE YOU AS A REVENGE MACHINE SO YOU COULD... HELP YOUR FRIENDS!
YEAH, BUT --
NO BUTS! YOU'RE GOING STRAIGHT TO STICATHA AND YOU'RE GOING TO GET REVENGE ON THE WITCH WHO KILLED YOUR FATHER AND THAT'S FINAL, YOUNG MAN!!

JUST LET ME EXPLAIN!
OH, HERA, IS THIS GOING TO BE ONE OF YOUR ENDLESS STORIES?
THEY'RE NOT ENDLESS -- THEY'RE EPIC!
MY ADVENTURES WITH BROAD-SHOULDERED PRAXIS AND QUICK-WITTED ATRUKOS WILL CONVINCE YOU OF THE NOBLENESS OF MY OATH!
KNOCK YOURSELF OUT. I MIGHT NOD OFF...
BUT IF I CONVINCE YOU, YOU HAVE TO LET ME GO!
HEH, YEAH, FINE. IF YOU CONVINCE ME.
BOING!

SO ONCE UPON A TIME, PRAXIS, ATRUKOS AND I WENT WANDERING OFF TO COMPLETE TWO QUESTS.
SPEED IT ALONG!
ATRUKOS' QUEST WAS TO RETURN A WITCH'S MAGIC EYE THAT HE'D STOLEN LONG AGO.
PIT PAT PIT
AN ORACLE TOLD HIM IT WAS THE ONLY WAY TO BREAK THE CURSE ON HIS APPEARANCE.
PRAXIS' QUEST WAS TO WIN THE HAND OF HIS LOVE, FAIR ECHINA.
TO PROVE HIS WORTH, HE HAD TO BRING HER A CHUNK OF SKY HE'D KNOCKED OUT WHILE FIGHTING A CYCLOPS.
FLING
ZOZIMOS!

WHAT?
GET TO THE POINT ALREADY!
OH. WELL...
WE WERE ON THE WAY TO RETURN THE EYE.
IN THE DISTANCE WE SAW A GREAT CRATER.
IT COULD ONLY BE ONE THING.
PRAXIS' CHUNK OF THE SKY.
ECHINA WILL BE IMPRESSED, RIGHT, GUYS? THAT I KNOCKED IT OUT OF THE HEAVENS?

IF I CAN GET IT ACROSS LAND AND SEA TO MY FAIR ECHINA... PERHAPS SHE'LL MARRY ME AT LAST!
THERE WE FOUND OUR OLD FOE, THE CYCLOPS.
BY NYX -- IT'S YOU! PLEASE DON'T HURT ME!
QUICK -- LET'S HURT HIM...
ZOZIMOS! I MUST INSIST WE TALK TO HIM FIRST!
AWW...
I'VE LEARNED MY LESSON.
EVER SINCE YOU FLUNG ME AGAINST THE SKY, I'VE BEEN TRAPPED, SURVIVING OFF ANY PASSING CREATURES THAT FALL INTO THIS CRATER.
CAN WE BELIEVE HIM? AND HOW ARE WE GOING TO GET THIS GIANT SKY CHUNK BACK TO ODONOROS?

I BELIEVE I HAVE AN IDEA! FOLLOW MY LEAD!
OH, I GET IT!
CYCLOPS -- WE WILL FREE YOU IF YOU SWEAR TO HELP PRAXIS DRAG THIS SKY-BOULDER TO HIS HOME ISLAND.
ANYTHING! ANYTHING! I'VE LEARNED MY LESSON!!
SO ATRUKOS PUT HIS CUNNING PLAN INTO ACTION, USING PRAXIS' GREAT STRENGTH.
I WAITED TO PLAY MY PART.
OH, THANK YOU! THANK YOU! NOW I WILL HELP YOU JUST AS I --
ATTACK!!
AAAAH! BETRAYERS!

HA HA HA! WHAT A CHICKEN!
HE WAS GOING TO HELP!
WHA?
THE PLAN WAS TO LURE HIM INTO LETTING DOWN HIS GUARD, THEN FINISH HIM OFF -- RIGHT?
THAT'S WHAT YOU MEANT, RIGHT? RIGHT?
I GUESS I'LL HAVE TO MOVE IT MYSELF.
YOU GUYS GO ON AHEAD -- I'LL CATCH UP!!

SO JUST ATRUKOS AND I JOURNEYED TO THE WITCH'S LAIR TO BREAK HIS CURSE...
I THOUGHT WE COULD JUST HAND IT OVER AND APOLOGIZE FOR EVERYTHING.
KNOCK KNOCK
HELLOOOOO, MISSUS WITCH! WE HAVE A PRESENT FOR YOU!
BUT SHE WOULDN'T ANSWER THE DOOR.
I HAD SWORN AN OATH TO HELP MY FRIENDS
CLANG
BUT THERE WAS NOTHING I COULD DO.
CLANG
CLANG

I DO NOT BELIEVE YOUR BRUTE FORCE ATTACK IS WORKING.
CRUMBS!
THIS IS MY FAULT. IF PRAXIS WERE STILL HERE...
DON'T OVERLOOK THE FACT THAT WE'VE BEEN IN TOUGHER SCRAPES...
NO!!
NO, I'M GONNA GO GET HIM!
FWOOP!
?
YOU MEAN PRAXIS? ZOZIMOS, WAIT! WE CAN DO IT OURSELVES!

NOT WANTING TO WASTE TIME, I MADE THE MONTHLONG TREK BACK TO THE CRATER...
SEE, THIS IS WHAT I'M TALKING ABOUT -- DILLYDALLYING!
ANYWAY...
I FOLLOWED THE DRAG MARKS FROM THE CRATER
...TO FIND PRAXIS LABORING AWAY.
ZOZIMOS! WHAT ARE YOU DOING HERE?
ATRUKOS NEEDS YOUR HELP TO GET INTO THE WITCH'S LAIR.
OKAY THEN, HELP ME COME UP WITH A FASTER WAY TO MOVE THIS THING!
NO PROBLEM -- I'LL ASK ATRUKOS.

YOU'LL ASK ATRUKOS...? ZOZIMOS?!
ZOZIMOS!!
YOU'RE PROVING MY POINT!! YOU HAVEN'T ACCOMPLISHED ANYTHING!
LET ME FINISH MY STORY!
FINE.
AHEM. I WAS JOURNEYING BACK TO ATRUKOS AT THE WITCH'S LAIR...
WHUMP

...WHEN YOU KIDNAPPED ME!
THERE. THE END. NOW I'M FINISHED.
THAT WAS SUPPOSED TO CONVINCE ME YOU SHOULD BE WASTING YOUR TIME INSTEAD HEADING STRAIGHT FOR STICATHA?!
YOUR FRIENDS ARE THE WORLD'S STRONGEST MORTAL AND THE WORLD'S SMARTEST FROG -- THEY DON'T NEED YOUR HELP!
ZOZIMOS, YOU NEED TO REMEMBER WHO YOU ARE.

REMEMBER THE STORY I USED TO TELL YOU EVERY NIGHT?
THE ONE ABOUT THE EVIL WITCH QUEEN WHO KILLED YOUR FATHER?
OF COURSE! IT'S BURNED INTO MY BRAIN!
IT TERRIFIED ME -- SHE NOT ONLY SEDUCED AND MURDERED MY FATHER BUT TURNED MY SISTERS INTO CROWS! IT COULD'VE BEEN ME.
SOMETIMES I WONDER WHERE THEY ARE.
LUCKILY, I SNUCK YOU AWAY AND TRAINED YOU TO BECOME A SKILLED WARRIOR!
IT'S IMPORTANT THAT YOU GET YOUR REVENGE AND RECLAIM THE THRONE...

...NOT FOR ME, BUT FOR THE PEOPLE OF STICATHA -- YOUR PEOPLE!
YOU'RE A KING, ZOZIMOS.
I KNOW... I WANT TO GO TO STICATHA MORE THAN ANYTHING IN THE WORLD!
BUT I FEEL KINDA WORTHLESS. MY FRIENDS ARE SO IMPRESSIVE!!
WITHOUT THEM, I NEVER WOULD HAVE GOTTEN THIS FAR...
RUSTLE!
RUSTLE!
THE KINGLY THING TO DO IS TO HELP THEM FIRST!!
RUSTLE!
THUD!
RUSTLE!

RUSTLE
RUSTLE
THAT'S DUMB. A KING DOES WHATEVER HE WANTS!
RUSTLE
RUSTLE
CRASH!
DO YOU HEAR THAT CRAZY RUSTLING?
CRASH!
UNTIE ME!!
CRASH!
THUD

SCREEE
UNTIE ME, NESTOR!
I'M BUSY -- UNTIE YOURSELF!
SNORT
UM...
I KNOW YOU'RE ALWAYS TRYING TO TEACH ME TO BE SELF-RELIANT, BUT HEEEEELP!!
RUMBLE RUMBLE
FINE, CRYBABY.

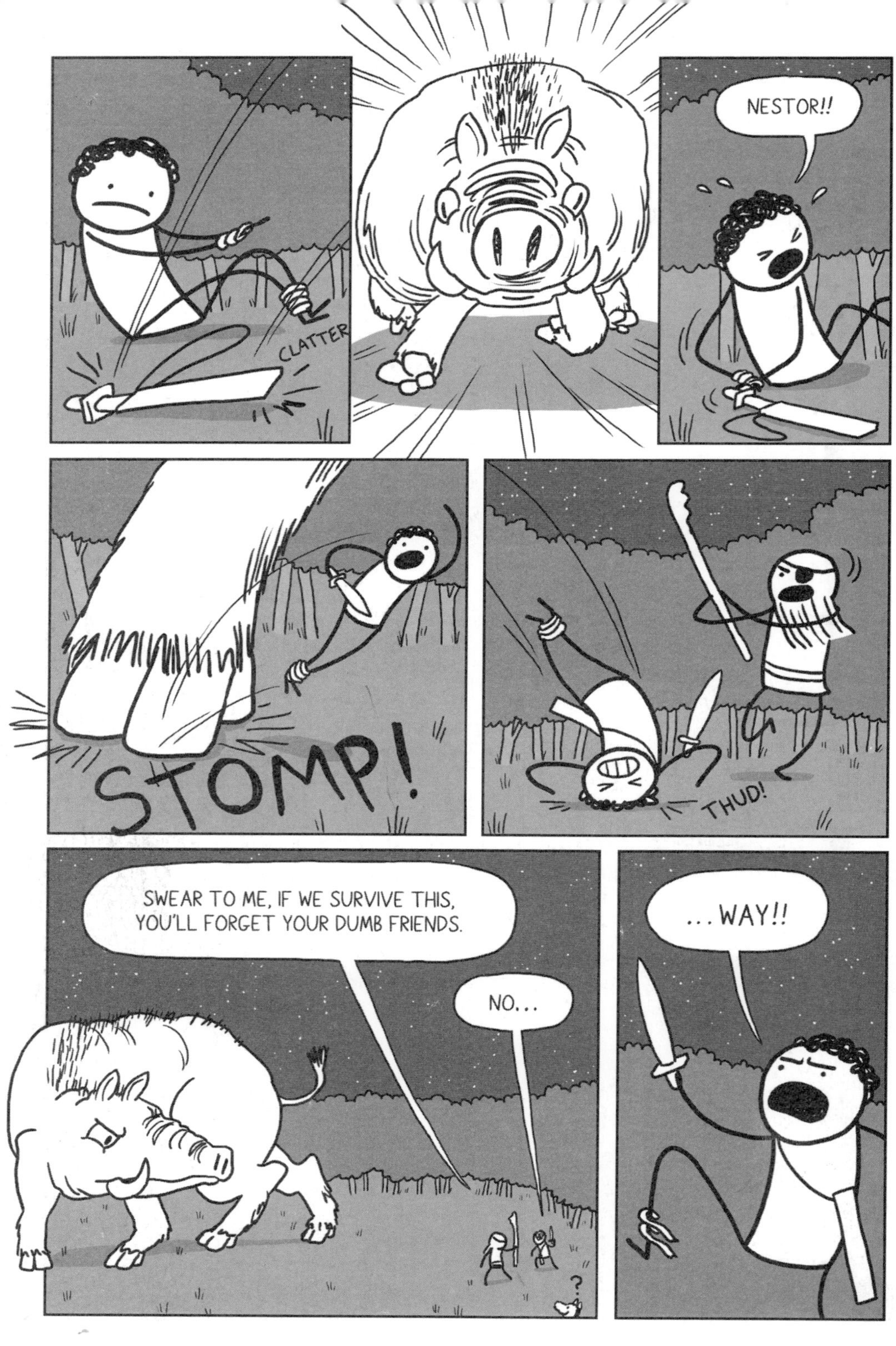
CLATTER
NESTOR!!
STOMP!
THUD!
SWEAR TO ME, IF WE SURVIVE THIS, YOU'LL FORGET YOUR DUMB FRIENDS.
NO...
?
...WAY!!

YAAAA!!
IDIOT.
EUREKA!
HEY, GIANT BOAR GOD --
OVER HERE, DUMMY!
AWW,
I WAS
HANDLING
THIS.

LOOK OUT, OLD MAN!
OH, HEAVENS!
FLUP!
NESTOR!
HE GOT ME, ZOZIMOS...

SNORT
HERE, LET ME HELP YOU!
NO. YOU HAVE TO FOCUS ON YOUR DESTINY NOW!!
SWEAR TO ME YOU'LL GO STRAIGHT TO STICATHA!
GET UP! HE'S COMING BACK!
RUMBLE RUMBLE
SWEAR IT!
AAH! I SWEAR IT!
STOMP
NOW GO -- STICATHA NEEDS YOU!
GASP

RUMBLE
CRASH
HEH HEH.
THAT WAS EASY.

THE NEXT MORNING
GET UP, STICK-MORTAL.
WHY? I'M WORTHLESS. I'M JUST GONNA LIE HERE.
GO BE WORTHLESS SOMEWHERE ELSE. THIS IS OUR HOME.

WHAT IN ZEUS' STOMACH FOLDS ARE YOU?
WE'RE DRYADS!!
THAT MEANS TREE SPIRITS, IN CASE YOU WERE TOO DUMB TO KNOW THAT.
I THOUGHT DRYADS WERE BEAUTIFUL MAIDENS.
TURNS OUT: NOPE.
YOU GOT A PROBLEM WITH THE WAY WE LOOK, CRUM-BUM?
MY ONLY PROBLEM IS THAT I'M LOST BECAUSE A GIANT BOAR KILLED MY UNCLE AND I'M NOT STRONG OR CLEVER, SO I'M JUST GOING TO LIE HERE.
LISTEN TO THIS WHINER...
YOU TELL 'EM, JERRY.

THAT BOAR IS THE GUARDIAN OF THE FOREST --
STICKMEN ARE FORBIDDEN HERE. HE WAS JUST DOING HIS JOB.
SO GET LOST. YOU'RE WORSE THAN WORTHLESS.
I'M NOT WORSE THAN WORTHLESS!
FWIP!
YOU GET LOST, YOU LITTLE JERKS!
POOT
I'M GONNA GET OUT OF THIS STUPID FOREST AND I'LL TELL YOU WHAT I'M GONNA DO RIGHT AFTER...
I'M GONNA TELL EVERYONE WHAT HORRIBLY UGLY LITTLE LUMPS DRYADS REALLY ARE.

HE JUST WENT OFF RIGHT TOWARD THE WATERFALL, RIGHT?
OH NO, YOU'RE RIGHT -- SHOULD WE WARN HIM?!
HA HA HA HA HA HA
FOOSH
SPLASH

HMM... A MYSTERIOUS MAIDEN BATHING IN A SECLUDED POOL IN A FORBIDDEN FOREST.
I'LL GO ASK HER FOR DIRECTIONS.
HEY, DO YOU KNOW THE WAY TO STICATHA?
SILENCE, MORTAL!! HOW DARE YOU TRESPASS HERE!
UH...
TURN AROUND!
I AM ARTEMIS, THE HUNTRESS GODDESS OF THIS FOREST AND ALL WILD THINGS, INCLUDING BEARS!

THERE. NOW FACE ME, MORTAL.
SHALL I MAKE YOUR PUNISHMENT AS SEVERE AS YOUR CRIME WAS BRAZEN?
JUST DO WHATEVER YOU'RE GONNA DO -- I'M A BUSY MAN!
I LIKE YOUR SPARK. I'LL GIVE YOU A *SPORTING* CHANCE.
GLORP!

UM... OKAY!
POP!
A GOAT!! I HATE GOATS.
BETTER RUN, YOU STUBBORN LITTLE THING. YOUR FRIEND IS COMING.
FLOOOO
TOUGH BREAK.

WHAT ARE YOU, SOME KIND OF MAGIC BIRD THAT TALKS?
?
THWIP!
ALEXA?!
ALEXA, MY LOVE! DON'T SHOOT -- IT'S ME, ZOZIMOS. I'VE BEEN CURSED!
I NEVER SEEN A BUCKLING SO BOLD!!
IT'S AS IF YOU WANT TO BE HUNTED -- AND SACRIFICED.

AAH!! NO, WAIT, WHAT ARE YOU DOING!
THWIP!
YOU'RE CRAZY! CAN'T YOU HEAR ME?
WHAT A GOAT! I MUST BRING HIS HEAD BACK TO MY MOTHER!
UH-OH.
SCREEE

CRASH!
THE GUARDIAN --
I SHOULDN'T BE HERE!
YOU WANNA FIGHT? I DON'T CARE HOW BIG YOU ARE!
I WON'T HURT YOU, LITTLE GOAT.
WHOA WHOA WHOA! YOU CAN TALK TOO?
OOOOH. YOU'RE ANOTHER ONE OF ARTEMIS' PRANK VICTIMS!!
SNIF
SNIF

SO WHAT IF I AM...
I GOTTA GET YOU OUT OF HERE -- FOLLOW ME.
HEY, WAIT -- YOU KILLED MY UNCLE!
I DON'T KILL STICKMEN. I JUST SCARE THEM AWAY FROM ARTEMIS' STOMPING GROUNDS.
SHE'S DANGEROUS!
RUMBLE
RUMBLE
BUT YOU DID -- YOU KILLED HIM!
I'M SORRY!! YOU STICKMEN ARE SO VERY TINY, SOMETIMES IT'S HARD TO TELL!

HE WAS A JERK, BUT HE WAS THE ONLY FAMILY I HAD LEFT!!
DONK
I'M SO SORRY! WHAT A TERRIBLE, CLUMSY MISTAKE! I'M SUCH A SIMPLETON!
YOU'RE NOT A SIMPLETON. YOU'RE A GIANT, TERRIFYING MONSTER!
THANKS. YOU'RE VERY BRAVE TO CHALLENGE ME AND ARTEMIS.
NO, I'M NOT BRAVE. I JUST LOSE MY TEMPER.
AH, HERE WE ARE -- THIS PATH WILL LEAD YOU TO YOUR STICATHA.

GREAT, BUT I'M STILL A GOAT.
YOU JUST GO ON AHEAD. AND SORRY ABOUT YOUR UNCLE!
YEAH, WELL, SORRY DOESN'T FIX ANYTHING!
A GIANT LIKE THAT OUGHTA BE MORE CAREFUL.
WHOA... HEY, DID YOU DO THIS?
SNORT
OH, RIGHT. WELL, "SQUEE SQUEE SQUEE." THANKS!

DUM DEE DOO
DEE DUM!
ALL RIGHT!
THERE'S THE END!
OH NO...
IT'S THE GREAT DESERT!
WHAT'S THAT ON
THE HORIZON?!
IS THAT ALEXA?

WELL, IF SHE CAN CROSS THE DESERT, THEN SO CAN I!
3 DAYS LATER
UHHH... THIS WAS A TERRIBLE IDEA.
I'M SO THIRSTY.
ZOZIMOS.

ZOZIMOS,
IT IS I, ATHENA.
WORRY NOT.
WATER!!
DUNK
PWHA!
THIS IS VINEGAR!

OH, IS IT?
MY MISTAKE.
LET ME TRY AGAIN.
OH, ATHENA, YOU'VE ALWAYS BEEN SO HELPFUL TO ME.
WOW! AN OASIS!
HA HA -- THAT WAS SO FUNNY BEFORE WHEN YOU MADE THE FOUNTAIN VINEGAR!
SPLISH!
GLURK!

PHBBT --
WHAT ARE
YOU DOING?
PHOOT!
HA HA HA HA HA HA HA HA HA HA HA
THIS IS FUNNY? I THOUGHT YOU WERE HERE TO HELP ME IN MY QUEST FOR STICATHA!
AAAAAHHHH... COME ON, ZOZIMOS, CAN'T YOU TAKE A JOKE? I'LL STOP. I'LL STOP.
LOOK OVER THERE -- I'VE MADE YOU A WATERSLIDE PARK!
WATER TOWN
IS IT VINEGAR AGAIN?

MAAAAAAAAAYBE YES.
MAAAAAAAAAAAYBE NO.
I'M IGNORING YOU NOW.
AW, COME ON. HERE, TAKE THIS JUG OF WATER.
I CAN'T HEAR YOU.
I'M WALKING OUT OF THIS STUPID DESERT ON MY OWN IF IT KILLS ME!!

NEVER LOSE THAT TEMPER OF YOURS, ZOZIMOS...
SHOOOO
STUPID BURNING HOT SUN!
STUPID ENDLESS DRY SAND.
STUPID PASSED-OUT WARRIOR PRINCESS.
ALEXA!

ARE YOU OKAY? SAY SOMETHING!
WATER...
DON'T WORRY --
YOU'RE COMING WITH ME!
I'M MAD ENOUGH
TO GET US *BOTH* OUT OF HERE!
STUPID VAST HORIZON!

THREE MORE DAYS LATER
STUPID THREE DAYS OF INTENSE SUFFERING!
THERE.
WHUMP
GLUG
GLUG
GLUG
AAAAHHH!
ZOZIMOS! THANK YOU. I THOUGHT I WAS DREAMING WHEN I SAW YOUR FACE.

ALEXA, MY LOVE, THE LAST TIME I SAW YOU, YOU SAID SOMETHING ABOUT...
STICATHA!
YES! STICATHA -- THAT'S WHERE I'M FROM.
ME TOO!
BUT I CAN'T FIND IT -- I'VE SEARCHED MY WHOLE LIFE.
ZOZIMOS! IT'S RIGHT OVER THERE!

SMOOCH
THIS IS ALL SO AMAZING! EVERYTHING'S TURNING AROUND! AND YOU -- A STICATHA GIRL!
YES, AND MY MOTHER IS THE QUEEN.
WAIT! WHAT? THE EVIL WITCH QUEEN?!
EVIL WITCH QUEEN? I MEAN, SHE HAS MAGIC POWERS...
SHRUG

THIS IS MY WHOLE THING! MY UNCLE RAISED ME TO SEEK REVENGE AGAINST THE WITCH QUEEN!
STOP CALLING HER THAT! MY MOTHER'S NAME IS KRATA.
SHE KILLED MY FATHER AND STOLE HIS THRONE!
MY MOTHER WOULDN'T DO THAT! THOUGH SHE NEVER WOULD TELL ME HOW MY FATHER THE KING DIED.
WELL, THAT PROVES IT -- WAIT -- DID YOU SAY FATHER?
YEAH, MY FATHER WAS THE KING. HE LOST HIS FIRST WIFE AND REMARRIED MY MO -- OH, HERA'S UNDERPANTS!!

YOU'RE MY --
WE'RE --
AAARRG!!
SCRUB
SCRUB
WE CAN NEVER LOOK UPON EACH OTHER AGAIN, ZOZIMOS! YOU PROMISE ME? NEVER AGAIN!
OKAY, ALEXA, BUT WAIT --

AND SO ZOZIMOS ENTERED STICATHA IN DISGUISE.
YOINK
IT'S SO NICE HERE, JUST LIKE NESTOR ALWAYS SAID.
BUT SURELY THE EVIL WITCH QUEEN'S OPPRESSION OF MY PEOPLE HAS TAKEN ITS TOLL...

HELLO, TRAVELER. WELCOME TO STICATHA!
ARE YOU THIRSTY?
UH... SORT OF. SO THIS IS REALLY STICATHA?
GET OUR GUEST SOME WATER, DEAR.
YES, THIS IS STICATHA, HAPPIEST KINGDOM IN ALL OF ZEUS' ISLES!
HAPPIEST?
BUT WHAT ABOUT THE OPPRESSIVE WITCH QUEEN'S TYRANNY?
QUEEN KRATA? SHE'S THE BEST!
WE LOVE HER!

PSSHT!
BUT, BUT HOW CAN YOU -- BUT SHE -- WHAT ABOUT THE OLD KING, MY FA-- I MEAN WHAT ABOUT OLD KING ZENON?
OH, HIM! HE WAS A NASTY OLD GUY. KRATA'S MUCH BETTER.
THANKS FOR THE WATER.
WHAT WAS THAT GUY'S PROBLEM?
AND WHY IS HE WEARING A SHEET?

HELLO, TRAVELER. WELCOME TO STICATHA!
THANKS. YEAH. GREAT.
WHAT'S WRONG WITH THESE PEOPLE? MAYBE KRATA'S GOT 'EM BEWITCHED?
SMILE!

HELLO, TRAVELER.
BACK OFF.
...WHICH IS WHY WE ALL SHOULD THANK OUR QUEEN KRATA FOR HER GENEROSITY!
WHAT ABOUT OLD KING ZENON!

WHO SAID THAT?
DIDN'T ZENON HAVE A LOST SON AND HEIR -- ZOZIMOS?
I NEVER HEARD THAT.
WHO CARES?
DUMB NAME.
EVERYBODY SHUT YOUR GOBS!
SHOVE!
I AM ZOZIMOS, SON OF ZENON!
FLUTTER
?
?
?

I'M YOUR RIGHTFUL RULER -- NOT THAT MURDERING WITCH KRATA!
HEY, THAT'S TREASON!
I'M SURE QUEEN KRATA CAN HELP THIS YOUNG FOOL.
BEHOLD, I CARRY MY FATHER'S ROYAL SWORD!
SWOO
WHOA, HEY, WHAT ARE YOU GONNA DO WITH THAT?
MAYBE I'M GONNA KILL KRATA WITH IT!
OKAY, PUT THE SWORD DOWN, BUDDY.

DON'T TELL ME WHAT TO DO!
!
SWIPE!
I'M GONNA STORM THE CASTLE! FOLLOW ME, STICATHANS!
FREEEEEEEEDOM!!
FREEEEDOM!
HEY, YOU CAN'T GO UP THERE!

THIS IS MY KINGDOM!
SHE STOLE IT AND KILLED MY FATHER!
CLANG
SHE TURNED MY SISTERS INTO CROWS!
SWIPE
AND SHE KILLED MY UNCLE NESTOR -- BASICALLY.
KICK
AND SHE'S RUINING MY KINGDOM AND MY PEOPLE!
I MEAN SERIOUSLY -- WHO SAYS "SMILE"?

SO YOU'RE ZENON'S CHILD.
I KNEW THIS DAY WOULD COME.
GET OUT OF MY CHAIR!
WHERE'S YOUR UNCLE NESTOR? I ASSUME HE PUT YOU UP TO THIS.
HE'S DEAD, ALL RIGHT? AND IT'S YOUR FAULT!

I SEE I HAVE NO CHOICE BUT TO DESTROY YOU.
AHA -- MAGIC! YOU ARE A WITCH.
THUD!
OW!
CRACK
WHUMP!
CRASH

BOOP!
CLANG!
IF ONLY YOU COULD ACCEPT THE TRUTH...
WHAT, THAT YOU'RE A BIG LIAR?
NO, THAT YOUR FATHER WAS A TYRANT.
BALONEY!
RIP!

NESTOR ONLY TOLD YOU ONE SIDE!
YOU'LL SEE HIM SOON ENOUGH IN HADES.
THE TRUTH IS NESTOR BETRAYED YOUR FATHER AS MUCH AS I.
HE ALWAYS WANTED THIS THRONE HIMSELF.
COME ON, LADY -- YOU THINK I WAS BORN YESTERDAY?!
IT'S TRUE I KILLED YOUR FATHER. BUT DO YOU KNOW WHY?!

WHAT? WHAT DO YOU MEAN --"WHY"?
YOUR FATHER LOVED WAR AND NESTOR WAS HIS GENERAL.
AS HE EXPANDED STICATHA'S BORDERS THROUGH BLOODY CONQUESTS...
...HE GREW JEALOUS OF MY HOME ISLAND -- THE ISLE OF WIZARDS.
ZENON'S ARMY INVADED, WIPED US OUT -- MY WHOLE FAMILY.
I HUNGERED FOR REVENGE. AND NESTOR FOUND ME.

HE PRETENDED TO BE A CONCERNED CITIZEN, BROUGHT ME TO STICATHA.
I HAD TO MARRY YOUR FATHER TO GET CLOSE ENOUGH. YOU WERE A BABY.
NESTOR THOUGHT I'D BE HANGED, LEAVING THE THRONE FOR HIM.
LUCKILY, I DISCOVERED WHO HE TRULY WAS AND FOILED HIS PLAN -- THOUGH HE ESCAPED WITH YOU.
I HELD ON TO THE THRONE TO SAVE MY LIFE. BUT AFTER MY REVENGE I FELT EMPTY.
WHEN ALEXA WAS BORN, I SAW HOW WRONG I HAD BEEN. I RAISED HER TO BE A WARRIOR FOR PEACE AND JUSTICE.
OOOOH, YEAH, RIGHT, ALEXA...

WHAT ARE YOU WAITING FOR?
OH NO! THE STATUES ARE COMING TO LIFE AGAIN!
NO, DUMMY -- IT'S ME!! KILL HER ALREADY!
YOU'RE ALIVE... ...OR A GHOST MAYBE?
YOU'RE SO GULLIBLE!
POKE
WHAT KIND OF AN UNCLE ARE YOU?

I'M THE KIND OF UNCLE WHO KNOWS WHAT'S BEST -- KILL HER!!
PLEASURE TO SEE YOU AGAIN, NESTOR.
QUIET, EVIL WITCH!
FORGET HER LIES. THIS IS YOUR DESTINY!
I KNOW. I KNOW. I'M DOING IT!
ZOZIMOS? ARE YOU IN HERE?

Y-YEAH?
ALEXA, WHAT HAPPENED TO YOUR EYES?
THAT IS NOT IMPORTANT NOW. I AM HERE TO ASK FOR PEACE!
PEACE! HA -- YOU'RE A TRAITOR TO YOUR OWN FATHER!
CLAK!
BUT YOU'RE BLIND!
CLAK!
YOUR ATTACKS ARE SO CLUMSY -- I CAN SMELL THEM COMING!!
CLUNK!

STOP FIGHTING! THIS IS MY THING!
YOU SEE, ZOZIMOS... THERE'S NO END TO IT.
YES THERE IS -- IF I KILL YOU, I GET MY KINGDOM BACK!
GO AHEAD, BOY. I'LL HANDLE THIS ONE.
ZOZIMOS, NO! YOU DON'T HAVE TO DO THIS!!
YOU DIDN'T HAVE TO KILL MY FATHER!
YOU DIDN'T HAVE TO TURN MY SISTERS INTO CROWS!!

...WAIT, WHAT SISTERS ARE YOU TALKING ABOUT?
COME ON -- REALLY?! MY SISTERS YOU TURNED INTO CROWS!
YOU WERE AN ONLY CHILD, ZOZIMOS.
NESTOR -- TELL HER ABOUT MY SISTERS!
UH... THEY WERE... UH, I MAY HAVE EMBELLISHED YOUR STORY A LITTLE!
SWIP

AWW! I DON'T HAVE SISTERS.
AWW...
SO GULLIBLE. WHAT DIFFERENCE DOES IT MAKE?
WHAT IF -- WHAT IF I DON'T KILL YOU?
CAN I HAVE MY KINGDOM BACK, PLEASE?
WELL, BECAUSE YOU ASKED NICELY -- YES, YOU MAY.
REALLY?!
?

ON ONE CONDITION!
OH, YEAH -- HERE WE GO.
THWAAK
OW! WE STOPPED FIGHTING!!
OH.
I CANNOT GIVE YOU THE THRONE IF YOU'RE ANOTHER WARMONGER LIKE ZENON OR NESTOR!
I'M NOT A WARMONGER -- I'M SUPER LAID-BACK!
TO PROVE YOUR WORTHINESS TO BE THE KING OF STICATHA -- YOU MUST COMPLETE A DANGEROUS QUEST!

ZEUS' FOOT FLAPS! MORE ADVENTURES?!
YOU DON'T HAVE TO TAKE ORDERS FROM *HER*!!
WELL... JUST HOW DANGEROUS ARE WE TALKING ABOUT?
YOU MUST SAIL TO THE EDGE OF THE WORLD, WHERE YOU MUST FIND THE GOLDEN FEATHER -- WHICH HOLDS THE POWER OF THE GODS...
MORE SAILING! NOT SO BAD. WHAT ELSE?
SLAP!
THEN YOU MUST BRING IT BACK TO ME!

DOESN'T SOUND TOO DANGEROUS.
DON'T FALL FOR HER TRICKS, ZOZIMOS.
OH, RIGHT -- I'M MR. GULLIBLE!
I THOUGHT YOU WERE DEAD!
I HAD TO TRICK YOU! IT WAS TOO IMPORTANT!
?
THEN COME WITH ME! HELP ME FIND THE GOLDEN FEATHER.
YOU'D REALLY HAND OVER THE POWER OF THE GODS TO HER!
IF YOU'RE TOO WEAK -- I'LL TAKE THIS THRONE BACK MYSELF!
?

YOU NO LONGER HAVE THE STRENGTH.
BUT UNLIKE YOU MORONS, I HAVE MY WITS! I'LL BE BACK IN ONE YEAR WITH AN ARMY LARGE ENOUGH TO CRUSH YOU!!
ONE YEAR!!
NESTOR -- WAIT!
YOU'LL HELP ME SAIL TO THE EDGE OF THE WORLD, RIGHT... SIS?

OF COURSE, ZOZIMOS -- AS MUCH HELP AS ONE BLIND SAILOR CAN BE TO ANOTHER!
ME, OH!
YOU PUT OUT YOUR EYES AS PENANCE, TOO, RIGHT?
OH, UH, YEAH... YEAH, OF COURSE. I ALSO STABBED OUT MY EYES -- AND NOW WE'RE COOL, RIGHT?
RIGHT... BROTHER!!
MOOOOM -- CAN WE USE YOUR SHIP? THE SUPER-FAST ONE?
OF COURSE, SWEETIE. AND YOU SHOULD TAKE ALONG THE GREATEST HEROES TO SERVE AS YOUR CREW!

THE GREATEST HEROES...

PART TWO

WHY COULDN'T WE GET TWO OF THESE THINGS?

MEANWHILE...
STILL NOT TALKIN', LIL' FROGGIE?
I TOLD YOU -- I DON'T HAVE YOUR EYE, I'D GIVE IT TO YOU IF I COULD!!
TOUGH TALK FER A FROGGIE IN A CAGE.
PLEASE LET ME GO! I CAN GET YOUR EYE BACK! JUST DON'T EAT ME!!
YEE-HEE HEE HEE HEE!

ALSO MEANWHILE...
FWOOF!
NOW TO FLOAT THIS FALLEN CHUNK OF THE SKY ACROSS THE OCEAN TO MY HOME ISLAND OF ODONOROS AND PROVE MY WORTH TO FAIR ECHINA!
HURK!
FOOM!

GOOD ONE, BRAINIAC!
HA HA HA!
HA!
HA HA!
SIGH.
HA HA
HA HA
I GUESS I'LL NEVER MARRY MY SWEET ECHINA.
I MUST THEORIZE THAT I'LL NEVER LIVE TO SEE MYSELF FREE OF THIS CAGE.
SIGH.

CRASH!
ZOZIMOS! QUICKLY, LET ME OUT!
WAIT... HOLD ON... THAT HURT MORE THAN I THOUGHT IT WOULD...
WHUMP!
THERE'S NO TIME FOR PRATFALLS, YOU TWO. THE WITCH WILL --
THE WITCH WILL WHAT? TURN YOU INTO A FROG?

YEE HEE HEE
GET IT? A FROG! HE'S ALREADY A FROG!
GOOD ONE. NOW BREAK HIS CURSE OR I'LL CUT YOU IN HALF!!
AND I'LL BEAT BOTH HALVES INTO A BLOODY PULP!!
GROSS! SO VIOLENT! ALL I WANT IS MY EYE BACK.
OH, RIGHT, THE EYE.
I FORGOT I HAD IT.
I HAD OFFERED TO HOLD THE EYE, BUT YOU INSISTED!

GOODIE!
GOODIE!!
HOW DO I LOOK?
LOOK? UH... WHAT ABOUT YOUR END OF THE BARGAIN?
ZAP
ZAP!
ZAP!
POP!
CHANGE HIM BACK ALL THE WAY!
I DID!!
I UN-SHRANK 'IM..
WHUMP!

YEAH, I'M BACK TO THE OLD ME. NICE AND TALL!
WHAT, YOU THOUGHT IT WAS MY FROGGIE FEATURES? I'M FROM FROGMAN ISLAND!
ALL THOSE MASKS JUST ADDED HEIGHT. I HATED BEING SHORT -- THAT'S WHY I ALWAYS CLIMBED MOUNTAINS!
THAT SOUNDS LIKE A *STRETCH* TO ME!
YEE-HEE HEE!!
OH, THEY GOT AWAY.

WE'RE TOO HEAVY --
I'M RUNNING OUT OF WIND!
FOOSH
I THINK I SEE PRAXIS -- THERE, BY THE SHORE!
AND SO
...THEN IT SANK AND ALL THE NEREIDS LAUGHED AT ME.
THOSE SLIPPERY JERKS!
HEY, MERMAID SCUMBAGS! YOU LAUGH AT MY FRIEND'S MISFORTUNE?
HE'S ON A QUEST FOR LOVE, YOU WATERY WITCHES!

FOR LOVE!
AWW, WE FEEL BAD NOW.
YOU SHOULD FEEL BAD! WHAT'RE YOU GONNA DO ABOUT IT, THOUGH?
THAT'S RIGHT, LADIES -- PUT YOUR TAILS INTO IT!
IT FEELS GOOD TO HELP THESE SAILORS...
...INSTEAD OF JUST EATING THEM LIKE WE NORMALLY DO.
WHO KNEW?

AND SO THEN
OH, PRAXIS! IT'S BEAUTIFUL!!
YOU FINALLY DID SOMETHING RIGHT, DUM-DUM!
SO YOU'LL MARRY ME!
WE'LL BE TOGETHER FOREVER, MY LOVE!!
ZOZ, I HAVE TO COMMEND YOU -- DESPITE EVERYTHING, YOU KEPT YOUR PROMISE AND HELPED US BOTH.
HOW CAN WE EVER REPAY YOU?
WELL...

I KINDA NEED YOU TO GO ON ANOTHER ADVENTURE WITH ME.
ANOTHER ADVENTURE? BUT...
?
OF COURSE WE'LL GO WITH YOU, ZOZIMOS!
IT'S OKAY, PRAXIS!! HE WOULDN'T ASK UNLESS HE TRULY NEEDS YOU.
ALL RIGHT, ZOZ. WE'RE IN -- NOOGIES!
WHENEVER YOU LOOK AT THAT GAPING HOLE IN THE SKY, THINK OF ME! AND I'LL THINK OF YOU...

I CAN'T BELIEVE YOUR MAGIC BAG OF WIND RUNS OUT SO FAST.
IT'S MEANT FOR ONE.
IT'S FINE, ZOZ. THIS IS FUN!
I'M IMPRESSED YOU KNOW THE GUARDIAN OF THE FOREST!
JUST A LITTLE FARTHER, GUYS.
OKAY, THIS IS TERRIBLE.
MY MOM CAN REFILL MY WIND POUCH WHEN WE GET TO STICATHA...

HEY, WAIT. ISN'T THIS THAT STREAM WE DRANK FROM WHEN WE DISCOVERED TO OUR HORROR THAT WE'RE BROTHER AND SISTER?
IT IS -- WE'VE MADE IT BACK TO STICATHA!

NICE TOWN, ZOZIMOS. WHAT'S WITH THE HUGE WALL?
YOU'RE BACK! FINALLY!
AND THESE MUST BE YOUR HEROIC FRIENDS!
YOUR SHIP AND CREW ARE READY.
RIGHT THIS WAY.
SORRY TO BE SUCH A BAD HOST!
BUT RUMOR IS NESTOR'S SAILED TO THE ISLE OF THE CENTAURS TO RAISE AN ARMY!
OH, ALEXA, YOU'VE EMPTIED YOUR POUCH!
I'LL STEAL A LITTLE MORE WEST WIND!
HURRY DOWN TO THE DOCKS!
I'LL MEET YOU THERE IN A MOMENT.
OFF YOU GO.
WOW. SHE REALLY WANTS THAT GOLDEN FEATHER!

HERE IS YOUR SHIP -- THE STICOS.
AND YOUR CREW, THE STICONAUTS.
WE'LL GET THE GOLDEN FEATHER AND BRING IT BACK BEFORE NESTOR RETURNS!
AHOY, ZOZIMOS. I'M PEG-LEG. JOIN US IN THE TRADITIONAL STICATHAN SAILORS' CHEER --'TIS GOOD LUCK.
YAARRRR!
I'M BALDY.
AND I'M FATTY.
ARE YOU SHORTY?
MY NAME IS KYLE!

HEY, ZOZ, WHERE ARE WE GOING, ANYWAY?
OKAY, MEN, CUT THE LINES. RAISE ANCHOR!
SERIOUSLY. WHERE ARE WE GOING!!
UM... THE EDGE OF THE WORLD.
THE *WHAT* OF THE *WHAT*!

BUT SOON
WHY DIDN'T WE GET YOUR OTHER FRIEND -- THAT GIRL...?
OH, ASTERIA? SHE'S NO USE ON A DANGEROUS QUEST!
SHE'S JUST SOME SPOILED PRINCESS. PROBABLY DEAD BY NOW.
THAT'S HORRIBLE! I'M SURE SHE'S FINE.
WHATEVER.
WE'LL GET THE FEATHER IN NO TIME -- IT'S SMOOTH SAILIN'!
WAIT... WHENEVER I SAY THAT, SOMETHING TERRIBLE HAPPENS.

FOUR MONTHS LATER
WE'RE STARVING TO DEATH!
WE HAVE TO TURN BACK!
YOU THINK I'M NOT HUNGRY TOO?
I'M SO HUNGRY, ALL I'M POOPING ARE FARTS!
WHY DOES THIS ALWAYS HAPPEN? WHOSE JOB WAS IT TO PACK ALL THE FOOD?!
SMACK
YOU GUYS EAT TOO MUCH.

IT'S TRUE -- WE CAN'T KEEP GOING LIKE THIS.
AAAH -- IT FREAKS ME OUT THAT YOU CAN TOUCH MY SHOULDER.
WHAT ABOUT YOUR CRAZY FISHING TRICK, PRAXIS?
TOO HUNGRY... TOO WEAK...
ALEXA, WHAT DO YOU THINK WE SHOULD DO?
CAN'T YOU SMELL IT? WE'RE NEAR LAND!
SMELL IT? OH, RIGHT. YEAH, ME TOO. MY SENSE OF SMELL IS MUCH SHARPER THAN BEFORE --
-- WHEN I HAD EYES.

THUD!!
WE HIT SOMETHING!
ARE WE SINKING? IS IT A MONSTER?
SMELLS LIKE... THE EDGE OF THE WORLD.
BY ZEUS' WRINKLY KNEES --
WE'VE DONE IT!!

HEY, LOOK! SHEEP!!
?
FOOD!
DINNER!
ZOZIMOS, YOU SHOULD STOP THEM. WE KNOW NOT WHOSE ISLAND THIS IS -- OR WHOSE SHEEP!
ZOZIMOS?
?
SHEEP! DELICIOUS SHEEP!

AH, THIS IS THE LIFE. FOOD, FRIENDS, FIRE... BEAUTIFUL SUNSET.
WHAT ABOUT THE FEATHER?
WAIT FOR TOMORROW.
THE SUN IS SETTING AWFULLY CLOSE TO US!!
WHERE ARE MY LITTLE SHEEP FRIENDS?

UH... GO TALK TO HIM, PEG-LEG.
O MIGHTY HELIOS, SUN GOD, BRIGHT ONE, BRINGER OF LIGHT...
DID YOU DIM LITTLE MORTALS *EAT* MY BELOVED SHEEPIES?
YARRR... NO...
YOU'VE DONE IT! I CAN FEEL A MIGRAINE COMING ON!

FOOM!
ARG!
HELIOS!! CALM DOWN!
DARLING, GET BACK INSIDE THE CHARIOT -- I'M HANDLING THESE KNAVES.
NOW, HELIOS, REMEMBER WHAT WE TALKED ABOUT? YOUR BLOOD PRESSURE?
I KNOW, DARLING. BUT THESE MORTALS --
THEY'RE MY FRIENDS.
WHOOSH!

FRIENDS?!
YES, ZOZIMOS. IT'S ME.
ASTERIA!
BUT YOU -- WHAT ARE YOU DOING HERE?!
THUP!
I'M DATING HELIOS. WHAT ARE YOU DOING HERE?
FLIRP!
UH...
HELIOS, HUN. TIME FOR BED. YOU GOTTA BE UP EARLY!
YES, DEAR.

ALTHOUGH, BETWEEN YOU AND ME, DATING HIM IS MORE LIKE BABY-SITTING.
LET THE FEASTING CONTINUE!
SO TELL ME EVERYTHING! I CAN'T BELIEVE IT'S YOU!
I TRAVELED FOR A WHILE. I'VE SEEN THE WHOLE WORLD FROM ATOP HELIOS' CHARIOT...
WOW, REALLY?

YEAH -- LIKE YOU, LOST IN THE GREAT DESERT, DRINKING ATHENA'S VINEGAR!
HA HA HA!
THAT WASN'T FAIR! SHE TRICKED ME!
YOU GOTTA LEARN HOW TO HANDLE THE GODS, ZOZIMOS.
LIKE ME -- I GOT ARES THE GOD OF WAR TO TEACH ME TO BE A WARRIOR.
SHRIK
WHAT, YOU A WARRIOR? HA HA -- PLEASE!
WANNA SPAR?
I DON'T WANT TO HURT YOU.
OOF!
BONK!

CLANG!
FLIP!
NICE MOVES!
ENOUGH!
WHAT'S WRONG, ALEXA?
UH, SOMEBODY...
MIGHT GET HURT.

SO HOW ABOUT YOU, ZOZ? WHAT'VE YOU BEEN UP TO?
OH, YOU KNOW. SO MANY THINGS. DID YOU KNOW DRYADS DON'T LOOK LIKE BEAUTIFUL MAIDENS -- THEY LOOK LIKE HORRIBLE LITTLE SICK POTATOES!
I DIDN'T KNOW THAT. BUT WHAT BRINGS YOU TO THE EDGE OF THE WORLD?
OH! THAT'S RIGHT -- YOU CAN HELP ME! I'M HERE TO FIND THE GOLDEN FEATHER.
ZOZIMOS, THE GOLDEN FEATHER IS AT THE *OTHER* EDGE OF THE WORLD.

WHAT DO YOU MEAN BY "THE OTHER EDGE OF THE WORLD"?
UH-OH, ZOZIMOS. WE ONLY HAVE SIX MORE MONTHS UNTIL NESTOR INVADES!
ACCORDING TO MY CALCULATIONS, TO SAIL TO THE OTHER EDGE OF THE WORLD ALONE WOULD TAKE AT LEAST THREE --
THREE *MONTHS*, RIGHT?! THEN WE COULD JUST MAKE IT!
THREE *YEARS*.

HEY, ZOZ!!
WHAT'S THE PLAN?
GO AWAY.
DON'T BE MAD AT YOURSELF.
I'M NOT MAD AT MYSELF -- I AM *FURIOUS!*
I ALWAYS *DO* THIS!
ZOZIMOS, THE CREW NEEDS TO KNOW WHAT YOU WANT TO DO.

I DON'T CARE.
I QUIT. I GIVE UP.
COME UP ON DECK, ZOZIMOS. THE SEA AIR WILL DO YOU GOOD.
NO.
ARE YOU POUTING DOWN HERE??
ASTERIA -- YOU'RE COMING TOO?

THEY WANT TO KNOW YOUR PLAN!
I DON'T HAVE A PLAN!
BUT ZOZIMOS --
STICATHA IS IN DANGER.
THEN YOU BE IN CHARGE!
IT'S YOUR KINGDOM TOO.

WE HAVE TO TRY!
I MAY HAVE LOST MY SIGHT...
BUT I NEVER GAVE UP. AND NEITHER WILL WE!
SET SAIL FOR THE OTHER EDGE OF THE WORLD!
YAAAAAR!
GREAT. FINE. WHATEVER.
HEY, ASTERIA -- WAIT UP.

SO I'VE BEEN THINKING, MAYBE, YOU KNOW... THE TIME IS RIGHT FOR US TO GIVE IT A SHOT!
I ONLY DATE AT LEAST DEMIGODS NOW.
BESIDES, YOU'RE DESTINED TO KILL ME WITH YOUR SWORD THERE.
I THINK WE SHOULD KEEP OUR DISTANCE.
SO, HEY, PRAXIS, WHAT'S UP?
CAN'T TALK NOW, ZOZ! TOO BUSY SETTING SAIL.
YOUR TALLNESS IS CREEPING ME OUT.

AND SO THEY SAILED ON
WITH NO HELP FROM ZOZIMOS.
HOW FAR HAVE WE COME?
NOT FAR ENOUGH!
AT THIS RATE, WE WON'T EVEN REACH THE OTHER EDGE OF THE WORLD BEFORE NESTOR HAS INVADED STICATHA...
I TOLD YOU -- THERE'S NO POINT, IT'S HOPELESS.
I HAVE A PLAN.
AN EXTREMELY DANGEROUS PLAN.

MY MOTHER REFILLED MY MAGIC POUCH WITH THE WEST WIND...
SO YOU'RE GONNA FLY AWAY, LEAVING US ALL TO OUR DEATHS!
NO! THE POUCH IS FULL. IF I LET ALL THE WIND OUT IN ONE BIG GUST...
THE WHOLE SHIP WOULD GO FLYING!
THAT'S CRAZY -- WE'D ALL BE BLOWN OFF!
WE HAVE TO TRY. OTHERWISE IT'S POINTLESS. YOU SAID SO YOURSELF.

EVERYONE READY?
SORTA!
...UM!
HERE WE GO.
WHOOSH
WHAAAAAAA!
I'M SLIPPING!

ASTERIA!
I GOT YOU!
WHOA! UH-OH!
GRAB ON TO ME!!
OKAY, THIS IS RIDICULOUS.
GOT YOU!
I'M TALL -- GRAB ME!
?

DAYS LATER
I THINK WE'RE SLOWING DOWN!
I GOT THE CRAMP-ARMS!!

SO WHERE ARE WE?
THANKS FOR JUMPING FOR ME, ZOZIMOS.
YOU WOULD HAVE DONE THE SAME FOR ME, RIGHT?
...DID WE MAKE IT TO THE OTHER EDGE OF THE WORLD?
SMELLS LIKE... CLOUDS!
WELL, HELLO THERE, WIND-STEALERS.

WHO ARE YOU?
OH MY, WHAT A RAVISHING CREATURE YOU ARE!
DON'T YOU KNOW ME? I'M THE RIGHTFUL OWNER OF THAT GUST YOU WASTED -- ZEPHYRUS, THE WEST WIND!
I'VE BEEN OVERLOOKING THAT SORCERESS KRATA SKIMMING MY POWER FOR TOO LONG.
BUT NOW MY WINDS HAVE BROUGHT YOU TO ME SO THAT I MIGHT BLOW YOUR SHIP APART.
WE MEANT NO HARM!
OH, DON'T YOU WRINKLE YOUR DELIGHTFUL BROW, MY LITTLE BEAUTY! I'M FAR TOO SMITTEN WITH YOU TO BE SO DESTRUCTIVE!

HEY! THAT'S MY SISTER YOU'RE TALKING TO, BUDDY.
OH, BUT THIS WILL NEVER DO WITH ALL THESE SAILORS ABOUT!
COME WITH ME TO MY PRIVATE LITTLE ISLAND, MY BEAUTY...
ALEXA!
WHOOSH
SHOULD WE GO AFTER HER?
OR SHOULD WE CONTINUE TO THE OTHER EDGE? WE'RE RUNNING OUT OF TIME!

I DON'T KNOW! WHO'S IN CHARGE HERE, ANYWAY?
NO WAY, NOT ME! I ALREADY PROVED I ALWAYS MAKE THE WRONG DECISION!
...SHE WOULD PROBABLY WANT US TO KEEP GOING.
BUT WE CAN'T JUST LEAVE HER!
IT'S IMPOSSIBLE! WHO'S GOT A COIN?
COME ON, I'LL PAY YOU BACK!

I HOPE YOU KNOW WHAT YOU'RE DOING.
I DON'T -- THAT'S THE WHOLE POINT.
HEADS, WE KEEP GOING.
TAILS, WE GO AFTER ALEXA.
WELL, WHAT'S IT SAY?!
HERE'S YOUR COIN.

WE GO AFTER HER. SET SAIL DUE WEST.
YAARRRR!
SO, GOING AFTER ALEXA. WAS THAT HEADS OR TAILS?
UM... IT WAS, UH...
ZOZIMOS, YOU'VE CHANGED --
FOR THE BETTER!

WELL, WELL, WELL. THE UNRULY SAILORS DON'T KNOW WHEN TO GIVE UP.
WE'LL NEVER LEAVE UNTIL YOU GIVE ALEXA BACK!
HAVE YOU CONSIDERED SHE DOESN'T WANT TO GO BACK ON YOUR CREAKY LITTLE SHIP? MY ISLAND IS QUITE DELIGHTFUL.
YEAH, RIGHT. I BET IT'S BORING AND STUPID!
I CANNOT HAVE THIS! I INSIST YOU COME ASHORE AND SEE FOR YOURSELF WHAT YOU ARE MISSING.
FLOOSH

SEE HOW I TRICKED HIM INTO LETTING US IN?
FLOOSH!
?
WHERE'S THE SHIP?!
I THINK ZEPHYRUS JUST TRICKED YOU BACK.
LABYRINTH, EH? NO PROBLEM. I BROUGHT SOME THREAD.
HA HA, AWESOME -- WE DOUBLE RE-TRICK HIM!
OKAY, SO... LEFT UP HERE?

HOURS LATER
UGH. THIS IS TAKING *FOREVER*, RIGHT?!
WHAT'S GOING ON HERE?!
THIS IS OUR THREAD!
TWANG!
HE'S CHEATING! HE'S CHANGING THE MAZE!
WELL, THE WALLS DO SEEM TO BE MADE OF CLOUDS!

HE'S A CHEATER!
FOOSH!
HE'S A ROTTEN, LYING CHEATER!
SWOOSH
ALEXA!
ZOZIMOS!
YOU SHOULD HAVE GONE ON WITHOUT ME!

BUT I'M GLAD YOU DIDN'T!
HA -- IT'S GOOD TO SEE YOU.
SEE ME?
UM, I MEAN --
HOW DID YOU GET THROUGH THE LABYRINTH, BLIND AS YOU ARE?
BLIND?
ER, I HAVE SOMETHING TO CONFESS... I MAY NOT HAVE ACTUALLY, TECHNICALLY GOUGED OUT MY EYES WITH YOU...
WHAT?

SMACK
OW! HEY!
YOU WERE SUPPOSED TO MAKE PENANCE WITH THE GODS!
HEE HEE HEE!
GOOD SHOW. ZOZIMOS -- I LIKE YOUR STYLE! YOU REMIND ME... OF ME! I'LL LET YOUR FAIR SISTER GO.
WHAT IS THIS -- ARE YOU TRYING TO DOUBLE RE-RE-TRICK ME BACK?
TO PROVE MY FOND AFFECTIONS, I'LL GRANT YOU A WISH...
GO AHEAD!
UM, ZOZ --
I WISH WE WERE ALL BACK ON THE SHIP, ARRIVING AT THE OTHER EDGE OF THE WORLD!

WHOOSH!
FWOOSH!
AND SO
SPLASH!
THE FAR EDGE OF THE WORLD -- WHAT A HORRIBLE PLACE!

BRRRR, IT'S COLD.
UM, ZOZIMOS...
YOU COULD HAVE JUST WISHED
FOR THE GOLDEN FEATHER.
WHAT'S MY PROBLEM?!
YOU SEE, ZOZIMOS,
THIS IS WHAT HAPPENS WHEN
YOU DON'T MAKE PENANCE.
IT'S OKAY, ZOZIMOS. IT'LL BE
MORE OF AN ADVENTURE THIS WAY!

I JUST WANNA DO SOMETHING RIGHT FOR ONCE...
BUT IF YOU HADN'T GONE THE WRONG WAY FIRST...
WE NEVER WOULD HAVE RE-MET!
ASTERIA... I'M SORRY ABOUT HOW I --
AHEM!
WELCOME TO THE ISLE OF NIGHT. I AM NYX, GODDESS OF DARKNESS.
WHERE'S THE GOLDEN FEATHER? HAND IT OVER!

DO NOT DARE TO BARK ORDERS AT ME, MORTAL. I AM NOT IN THE HABIT OF SUFFERING FOOLS, OR COLLECTING FEATHERS.
WHAT? OH, MAN! ARE YOU SURE?!
ZEUS DOES FORCE ME TO KEEP SECURE HIS MAGIC GARDEN IN THE CENTER OF MY ISLE, WHEREIN LIVES A GOLDEN *BIRD* OF QUESTIONABLE SAGACITY.
THAT'S GOTTA BE IT! HOW DO WE GET THERE?
THAT I CANNOT SAY. AT YONDER CROSSROADS YOU MUST CHOOSE YOUR OWN FATE.
ONE GUARD ALWAYS LIES. FOLLOW HIS ROAD AND YOU WILL BE LED TO THE UNDERWORLD, THE LAND OF THE DEAD.

THE OTHER GUARD IS IMPELLED TO TELL ONLY THE TRUTH.
DOWN HIS PATH YOU WILL FIND ZEUS' HORRIBLE LITTLE GARDEN.
YOU MAY ASK OF THEM BUT ONE QUESTION ONLY.
AHA -- A PUZZLE!
LET'S SEE... IF WE ASK IF THEY GUARD THE *GARDEN* PATH, THEY WILL EACH SAY YES, BUT --
DUNK
DOES THAT HURT?
DOESN'T HURT A BIT!

SO LET'S GO THAT WAY, RIGHT?
THAT METHOD ALSO WORKS.
THE PATH WAS NOT EASY.
I'VE NEVER BEEN SO COLD!
WHAT IS THIS STUFF?
DOES IT NOT SNOW IN STICATHA?
COME ON, STICONAUTS, A LITTLE COLD AND DARKNESS NEVER KILLED ANYONE!

I THINK WE'VE GOT TO BE CLOSE!
SO TIRED.
I THINK I'M GONNA GO TO SLEEP IN THIS PILE OF SNOW.
BALDY'S GOT THE RIGHT IDEA!
ZZZ
ZOZIMOS... LET'S STOP AND REST JUST A MOMENT!!
NO, KEEPING GOING, YOU LAZY JERKONAUTS!
ZZZ
ZZZ
ZZZ
ZZZ
ZZ

SHE'S RIGHT, ZOZ. IT'S NAP TIME!
WE'LL JUST REST OUR EYES... FOR A MOMENT.
I'M TIRED TOO, GUYS, BUT WE'RE SO CLOSE!
YAWN!
YES, ZOZIMOS. CLOSE YOUR EYES. I WILL TUCK YOU IN.

THANKS, NYX.
YOU'RE THE BEST.
WAIT A MINUTE!
YOU'RE THE WORST!
I'M TOO ANGRY TO SLEEP!
WAKE UP, PRAXIS. I GOT A PLAN!
MUSH! MUSH!
HIYA THERE! KEEP WALKING,
SLEEPER. MUSH!
Z Z Z
Z Z Z
Z Z Z
Z Z Z

KEEP WALKING. HIYA!
HUH? WHERE ARE WE?!
UGH! WHAT HAPPENED?
THIS HAS GOTTA BE IT!!
IT WOULD BE A WASTE OF YOUR TIME TO VENTURE FORTH.

YEAH, RIGHT -- YOU'RE A LYING LIAR FULL OF LIES!
I WILL FINALLY SHARE WITH YOU THE TRUTH.
ZEUS' GOLDEN BIRD IS *NOT* AT THE CENTER OF THIS GARDEN, WHICH IS *NOT* BEHIND THREE GATES --
-- WHICH ARE *NOT* EACH GUARDED BY A MONSTER THAT IS *NOT* MORE FEARSOME THAN THE ONE BEFORE.
I THINK THAT'S A DOUBLE NEGATIVE.
WE'RE GOING IN!
I WOULDN'T.

WAIT, THERE'S SOMEONE ON THE OTHER SIDE!
BY ZEUS' NAVEL, IT'S A GIANT WITH ONE HUNDRED UNBLINKING EYES!
QUITE AN INGENIOUS POSITION FOR A WATCHFUL MONSTER. I'D SURMISE THAT HE NEVER RESTS ALL EYES AT ONCE. THUS, ANY ATTEMPT TO SNEAK PAST HIM WOULD --
HEY, THAT GIVES ME AN IDEA!
SHOVE

ONE MORE MOVE AND I'LL SMASH YOU.
I SURMISE YOU MAY HAVE MADE AN INTERESTING MISSTATEMENT AND I WOULD LIKE TO VERIFY YOUR MEANING EXACTLY SO AS TO AVOID AN UNDUE SMASH. DO YOU MEAN *ANY* MOVE, EVEN IF THAT MOVE IS TO RETREAT FROM THIS FORBIDDEN GARDEN? IF SO --
LOOK, IT'S WORKING!
-- WHICH OF COURSE WOULD BE THE OPPOSITE OF THE PRESUMED MEANING; HOWEVER, I FIND THAT MUCH ON THIS ISLAND IS AT ODDS WITH --
FINISH HIM OFF, ATRUKOS!
ALLOW ME TO SUMMARIZE...

Z Z Z Z
WHUMP!
YARRRR!
ZZZ
SSSHHHHH!!
ZZZ
SO THIS IS ZEUS' GARDEN!
THE NEXT GATE AWAITS.
THESE STONES ARE CREEPY. THEY ALMOST LOOK LIKE PEOPLE.

LOOK, THE NEXT GUARDIAN.
NO, DON'T LOOK! IT'S A GORGON! GAZING ON HER FACE WILL TURN YOU TO STONE.
WHAT ARE WE GONNA DO?! IS SHE COMING OVER HERE?
I'LL HANDLE HER!

ALEXA, NO!
OH, WAIT... GOOD IDEA.
YARRR!
WHIFF
SSSSO, THE OLD BLINDFOLD ROUTINE...
LOOK UPON MY PRETTY FACE!
EW! GROSS!!

STAB!
CAN WE TURN AROUND?
ONE SECOND!
SPLOT!
KICK
OKAY, YOU'RE GOOD.
AYE, THAT'S SUPER GROSS.
NICE JOB!

ALL WHO ENTER HERE FACE THE MONSTER THEY BRING INSIDE
ANYONE SEE THE MONSTER THAT LURKS ON THE OTHER SIDE?
READ THE SIGN, ZOZIMOS.
ALL WHO ENTER HERE FACE THE MONSTER THEY BRING INSIDE
SO, TRYING TO BE ALL TRICKY AND IRONIC, HUH? LEMME IN THERE!
WAIT, ZOZIMOS, MAYBE SOMEONE LESS... *PRICKLY* SHOULD GO.
I'M PURE OF HEART. I'LL HANDLE THIS ONE.

HEY, GET BACK HERE!
AAAIIIII!!
WHAT WAS IT? WHAT DID YOU SEE?!
I SAW... I SAW...
THAT'S IT!

ZOZIMOS, NO!
HEY, YO -- BUDDY. COME OVER HERE.
?
YO -- PSSSST! WANT A GOLDEN FEATHER?

YEAH!
OKAY, I CAN HOOK YOU UP!!
BUT YOU GOTTA BATTLE THAT MONSTER YOU BROUGHT HERE!
WHAT MONSTER? MONSTROUS GOOD LOOKS?
NOPE. IT'S YOUR ANGER. YOU CAN'T CONTROL THAT TEMPER OF YOURS!
TEMPER? WHAT TEMPER!
HISSSSSSSSSS

CHECK IT OUT --
THE DRAGON OF WRATH.
HISSSSSS
FOOM!
HISS!
SLASH!
HISSSSSS

WOOP!
FOOM!
THUD
SURE YOU WANNA DO THIS, BUDDY?

YOU SURE YOU WANNA KILL YOUR WRATH?
SLORT!
POP!
THAT WAS AWESOME.

YOINK!
HERE YA GO.
REMEMBER -- IF YOU TALK TO ZEUS, YOU NEVER SAW ME.
YOU DON'T KNOW ME, I DON'T KNOW YOU.
THANKS!
WHAT'S TAKING SO LONG?
YARRRR!

SMOOCH!!
AHEM.
I AM GLAD, AT LEAST, THAT THAT HORRIBLE BIRD IS GONE.
YOU'RE WELCOME.
INDEED. NOW LEAVE MY ISLAND AS QUICKLY AS POSSIBLE.
DOWN THIS PATH LIES A SHORTCUT BACK TO YOUR SHIP. HURRY AND LEAVE ME TO MY DARK SOLITUDE.

YAY! SHORTCUT!
I'M SO PROUD OF YOU, ZOZIMOS.
IN WHAT WAY DOES THE GOLDEN FEATHER HOLD THE POWER OF THE GODS, DO YOU THINK?
I DUNNO. BUT NOW THAT I GOT IT...
AM I FANCY ENOUGH TO DATE YOU, ASTERIA?

HMMMMM...?
WHAT IS IT?
IT'S A TEMPLE OF SKULLS, YOU STUPID IDIOT!!
I'M BLIND, NOT STUPID! WHO ARE YOU?!
SHUT UP! YOU DON'T NEED TO KNOW MY NAME!

I RAISE THIS MIGHTY TEMPLE IN HONOR OF MY MOTHER, NYX.
WE WERE JUST LEAVING.
WHUMP!
NOT SO FAST, CURLY. EVERYONE WHO PASSES THIS WAY HAS TO WRESTLE ME.
AND EVERYONE WHO WRESTLES ME LOSES.
WELL, YOUR MOM TOLD US TO GO THIS WAY TO OUR SHIP, SO YOU CAN LET US PASS.
HEY, IDIOT -- WHAT PART OF "YOU HAVE TO WRESTLE ME" DO YOU NOT GET?!

I'LL WRESTLE YOU! LEAVE ZOZIMOS ALONE.
OKAY, FATSO, LET'S SEE WHAT YOU GOT!
I'M NOT FAT, I'M --
FOOF!
ZERP!

CRACK!
YOU WRESTLE LIKE A GIRL, FATSO!
HEY, YOU'RE A REAL PIG, YOU KNOW THAT!
HAR HAR HAR!
OKAY, CURLY, YOU CHOOSE WHOSE SKULL I RIP OUT FIRST!!

WHY NOT MAKE YOUR TEMPLE OUT OF ROCKS INSTEAD OF SKULLS?
WHAT? BECAUSE THAT WOULD BE LAME!
WOW -- YOU REALLY ARE AN ACTUAL IDIOT!
YOU'RE ENTITLED TO YOUR OPINION.
GO ON, ZOZ. STAB 'EM WITH YOUR SWORD!
THERE'S NO NEED TO STAB HIM. HE'S JUST A LITTLE CONFUSED.

WE CAN WORK THIS OUT, RIGHT?
?
WORK IT OUT? UH... UH... NO!
VERY CLEVER, ZOZIMOS! IT IS SAID THE SON OF NYX IS "STRIFE"!
HE GAINS STRENGTH FROM CONFLICT. GIVE HIM NOTHING BUT KINDNESS!
DO YOU WANT SOME HELP BUILDING YOUR TEMPLE?
WITH ALL OF US WORKING TOGETHER, WE COULD BUILD A NICE STONE ONE!

NO! NO! I DON'T WANT YOUR HELP!
WE CAN DECORATE THE TEMPLE WITH FLOWERS WHEN WE'RE DONE!
NO! GROSS! YOU'RE SO LAME!!
AWWWW, LOOK AT YOU NOW. YOU'RE SO CUTE!
YOU'RE LIKE A CUTE LITTLE BABY!
LOOK HOW CUTE STRIFE IS, EVERYBODY!

AWWWW!
POP
LET'S GO TO THE BOAT.
WHEREVER THAT LITTLE GUY IS NOW, I HOPE HE'S HAPPY.
?

AND SO
WAIT!
COME BACK! I *WON'T* KEEP TRYING TO KILL YOU ALL!
NICE TRY, NYX! YOU'RE HILARIOUS.
I'M BORED.

WE HAVE ONLY A FEW MONTHS TO GET TO STICATHA...
IF WE TRY OUR HARDEST, WE MIGHT JUST MAKE IT!
I'M GLAD YOU'RE OUT OF YOUR FUNK.
SMOOCH!
?
SMOOCH SMOOCH
IT MUST BE AN ODD SITUATION FOR YOU.

WHO, ME? WELL, IT IS A BIT OVERWHELMING.
WHEN I FEEL BAD, I CLIMB UP SOMEWHERE HIGH AND HAVE A GOOD LOOK AROUND.
OH -- SORRY. I DIDN'T MEAN "LOOK," I --
IT'S OKAY, I'M BLIND. I'LL LIVE.
I WOULD HAVE LIKED TO SEE YOU WITH YOUR CURSE BROKEN, THOUGH.
WANT TO CLIMB UP TO THE CROW'S NEST WITH ME?
I MEAN, TO CHECK ON THE SAIL -- WE HAVE TO TRY OUR HARDEST!

HEH, HOW'BOUT THOSE TWO?
FIRST ZOZIMOS AND ASTERIA. WHO'S NEXT?
I'M MARRIED TO THE SEA, MYSELF. HOW'BOUT YOU?
HUH? WHAT WAS THAT, PEG-LEG?
WHAT ARE YOU STARING AT, ANYWAY?
OH, NOTHING.

THREE MONTHS LATER
WOW. THAT WAS A LOT OF SAILING!
OH, STOP COMPLAINING, KYLE -- WE'RE ALMOST HOME TO STICATHA.
LAND HO!!
YOU SEE LAND?
NOT YET -- BUT ALEXA CAN SMELL IT!
SMELLS LIKE HOME!

LAND?!
THERE IT BE!
STICATHA!
WE'VE DONE IT!
WHAT'S THAT TO THE LARBOARD?
ARE YOU MESSING WITH ME, ATRUKOS?

IT'S AN ARMADA --
HEADED FOR STICATHA!
ALL RIGHT, MEN!
THIS IS IT! OARS OUT!
STROKE! STROKE! STROKE!
IT'S NO USE! WE'RE HOLDING STEADY WITH THEIR LEAD SHIP!

AHOY THERE, NEPHEW.
YOU REALLY DID IT! YOU RAISED AN ARMY!
GIVE ME THE GOLDEN FEATHER --
AND WE WILL RULE STICATHA AS UNCLE AND NEPHEW!

OTHERWISE, IT'S WAR!
WITH MY ARMY OF MERCENARY CENTAURS!
WHEN DO WE GET PAID, BY THE WAY?
NOT NOW.
I'LL NEVER JOIN YOU!
DON'T YOU SEE? THERE DOESN'T HAVE TO BE ANY MORE ANGER AND FIGHTING!
YOU THINK YOU'VE BECOME WISER THAN ME, *BOY?!*

YOU STILL WEAR MY BROTHER'S SWORD. YOU LIVE AND DIE FIGHTING LIKE THE REST OF US.
YOU'RE RIGHT.
I DON'T NEED IT ANYMORE!
WHAT ARE YOU DOING? THAT WAS SUPER EXPENSIVE! FISH IT OUT!
SPLASH
DON'T DO THIS, UNCLE. WE CAN LIVE IN PEACE!

NOT IF I GET THERE FIRST!
THROWING YOUR SWORD OVERBOARD GAVE ME AN IDEA.
SPLASH!
GET BACK HERE, YOUNG MAN!

SOON
RUN EVERYONE, RUN! NESTOR IS COMING!
EVERYONE INTO THE CITY GATES, BEHIND THE WALLS!
SPREAD THE WORD -- HURRY!
AND SO
CLOSE IT -- THAT'S THE LAST OF THEM!
CREEEAAK!

SLAM!
QUICKLY, TO THE WALLS! THEY HAVE NOWHERE TO RUN.
WHAT'S THE PLAN?
I NEED TO FIND KRATA.

I'M BACK AND SO IS MY CRAZY UNCLE!
YOU DID IT!
YOU HAVE THE FEATHER?
HERE YOU GO.

YOU HAVE TO USE IT OR SOMETHING!
NESTOR IS INVADING!
NESTOR!
AND SO
WE ARE SURROUNDED!
IF THE FEATHER HAS THE POWER OF THE GODS -- USE IT!

IT HAS GREAT POWER, BUT I ONLY MEANT YOU TO FETCH IT TO PROVE YOUR WORTHINESS.
BUT WHAT DOES IT *DO?*
THIS.
IT CAN DRAW ANYTHING TO LIFE, LIKE THE GODS.
WE MUST NEVER ABUSE THIS POWER, OR ZEUS HIMSELF WILL BECOME FURIOUS WITH DIVINE JEALOUSY.
DRAW ONLY FOOD, DRINK, MEDICINE.

COULD IT DRAW NEW EYES FOR ALEXA?
YES, ZOZIMOS. PEACEFUL ACTS OF KINDNESS ARE FINE.
ZEUS CARES NOT ABOUT THESE THINGS.
I CAN SEE YOU'VE QUELLED YOUR WRATH, ZOZIMOS. YOU'RE READY TO ACCEPT THE THRONE --
MOTHER?
THWACK
EVERYBODY DOWN!

ALEXA!
MOM!
KRATA! WHAT DO I DO?
OH, ALEXA!
ZOZIMOS!
WHAT?

YOU'RE IN CHARGE...
LET THE PEOPLE SEE YOUR RAGE! LEAD THEM IN BATTLE AGAINST NESTOR!
NO.
EVERYONE STAY CALM. WE DON'T NEED TO FIGHT -- WE'LL BE SAFE INSIDE THE WALLS OF STICATHA!
WE CAN WAIT OUT THE INVADERS PEACEFULLY -- WITH THIS!!

?
WE WILL FEAST AND OFFER SACRIFICES FOR QUEEN KRATA'S ROYAL FUNERAL.
HOORAY FOR KING ZOZIMOS!
IF I'M GOING TO BE KING...
...I'LL NEED A QUEEN!

PART THREE

ONE YEAR LATER

CAN YOU SAY "APPLE," ZOTIKOS?
MAPPLE!!
I'VE GOT THE WEEKLY REPORT IN, ZOZIMOS...
EVERYTHING'S PEACEFUL?
FOOD WAS DRAWN AND DISTRIBUTED ON SCHEDULE. UH... AND THERE WAS, UH...

THE MASKED RAIDERS AGAIN?
WE CAUGHT ONE.
WHEN IS ALEXA GOING TO LEARN?!
IT DOES NO GOOD TO SNEAK OUT OF THE WALLS AND ATTACK NESTOR'S ARMY!
THEY'RE VERY POPULAR WITH THE PEOPLE...
THEY'RE ENDANGERING EVERYONE -- INCLUDING THEMSELVES.
BRING THE ONE YOU CAUGHT IN HERE. MAYBE I CAN TALK SOME SENSE INTO HIM.

I'LL GO GET HIM.
ZOZIMOS, THIS CAN'T GO ON. YOUR PEACE POLICY IS GETTING US NOWHERE.
WE'RE SAFE AND HEALTHY -- FIGHTING NESTOR GETS US NOTHING.
DOES IT, ZOTIKOS?
NUTTIN'!
THERE'S MY MEN. BATH TIME FOR ZOTIKOS.
HELLO, HUN.

YOU DON'T THINK ALEXA'S RAIDERS ARE IN THE RIGHT, DO YOU, HUNNY?
THERE ARE SOME WHO WANT TO FIGHT.
BUT FOR WHAT?
FREEDOM.
DON'T YOU WANT YOUR SON TO BE FREE?

ZOZIMOS, I'VE GOT THE PRISONER.
PEG-LEG! YOU?! HOW COULD YOU BETRAY ME!
THE SAME AS YOUR OWN SISTER, ALEXA. I RISK MY LIFE FOR STICATHA.
YOU RISK *EVERYONE'S* LIVES -- WHAT IF NESTOR'S CENTAURS FOLLOWED YOU BACK TO YOUR SECRET PASSAGEWAY THROUGH THE WALL?
WOULD YOU FIGHT THEM THEN, ZOZIMOS, SIR?

I'M ASKING THE QUESTIONS, PEG-LEG.
WHERE IS THE SECRET PASSAGEWAY?
WHAT HAPPENED TO YOU, ZOZIMOS, SIR? THE FIRE 'TIS GONE FROM YOUR HEART! BEFORE, YOU WOULD HAVE LED THE CHARGE.
I'M DOING WHAT I HAVE TO DO FOR MY KINGDOM.
TELL ME WHERE THE SECRET PASSAGEWAY IS!
IF THE CENTAURS FIND IT -- STICATHA IS DOOMED.
OH, PEG-LEG... WHAT HAVE YOU GOTTEN YOURSELF INTO?

IT'S ALMOST DAWN.
YOU SURE THIS IS THE RIGHT PLACE, PEG-LEG?
SSSHHHH!!
POP!

ZOZIMOS!
ARREST THIS MASKED RAIDER!
THERE'S NO TIME FOR THAT, ZOZIMOS -- SHE'S HURT!!
ALEXA? WHAT -- WHAT DO YOU MEAN!?
ZOZIMOS...
THUD

NO...
ASTERIA!
ZOZIMOS...
ASTERIA, WHO DID THIS -- WHO?!

IT WAS THE PROPHECY...
IMPOSSIBLE -- I THREW MY FATHER'S SWORD INTO THE SEA! IT'S GONE!
NO. NO, NESTOR HAD IT -- HIS SHIPS MUST HAVE...
NESTOR.
IT'S OKAY! WE'RE GONNA PATCH YOU UP!!
NO, ZOZIMOS. KISS ME -- FOR WE'LL NEVER MEET AGAIN.

SMOOCH!
I NEVER SHOULD HAVE TAKEN YOU ALONG...
I'M THE ONE WHO STOWED AWAY, DUMMY! I DON'T REGRET IT.
BUT LET OUR SON LIVE FREE, ZOZIMOS.
DON'T REGRET A THING...
LET OUR SON...
LET ZOTIKOS...

WHERE ARE YOU GOING?

ZOZIMOS -- OH!
HE'S MAD.

SLAM

NEEESTOR!
FINALLY!
RUMBLE
RUMBLE
RUMBLE
CHAAARGE!!

FOOM
FOOM

CRACK!
BY ZEUS' BEARD, BOY!
WHAT HAVE YOU DONE?
YOU'RE DEAD.

BOOM!
ZEUS?!
GIVE IT A REST WITH THE GOLDEN FEATHER!
NOT FOR ZOZIMOSES.
YOINK
GULP
WENT A LITTLE OVERBOARD, DON'T YOU THINK?

THIS IS ALL YOUR FAULT!
LEMME AT 'IM!
I SEE YOU GOT YOUR WRATH BACK.
PROBABLY SHOULDN'T BE MAKING WEIRD DEALS WITH MAGIC BIRDS.
THIS FIRE SWORD IS PRETTY AWESOME, THOUGH -- I'LL LET YOU KEEP THAT.
BYEEE.
FART!

BUMF!

YOU'RE WEAK.
THWACK!
NESTOR...
GUESS WHAT -- I'M NOT GOING TO HELP YOU.
YOINK!
SWIPE

YOU DON'T DESERVE THAT SWORD -- YOU THREW IT AWAY!
CRASH!
YOU KILLED ASTERIA WITH THIS SWORD --
THUD
-- AND NOW I'M GOING TO KILL YOU!!
SNAP!
MAPPLE!

WHY DID YOU BRING ZOTIKOS HERE?
DADA!
...IF I KILL YOU... SOMEONE WILL JUST WANT REVENGE AGAINST ME...
YEAH! DON'T KILL ME!
...AND THEN MY SON WILL KILL THEM...
...AND THEN SOMEONE WILL KILL *HIM*...
YOU'RE JUST GETTING THIS? IT'S HOW THE WORLD WORKS!

THEN THE WORLD IS DUMB.
THERE'S EITHER TOO MUCH WRATH OR NOT ENOUGH!
I'M NOT GOING TO KILL YOU.
BUT YOU CAN KILL ME IF YOU FEEL THAT YOU HAVE TO.
CLANG!

ATRUKOS, DON'T.
THIS IS BETWEEN ME AND NESTOR.
IF NESTOR CAN'T CONTROL HIS OWN WRATH -- THEN FINE.
JUST NO ONE AVENGE ME, OKAY!
ZOZIMOS, PLEASE!
I'M SERIOUS -- NO ONE AVENGE ME. OTHERWISE I'M LETTING HIM KILL ME FOR NO REASON.

OKAY, SO IF YOU'RE WRATHFUL ENOUGH TO STRIKE ME DOWN --
ME, TOTALLY UNARMED. LOOKING YOU RIGHT IN THE EYE... GO AHEAD.
CLANG!
HEY! I SAID THIS WAS BETWEEN ME AND NESTOR!! CUT IT OUT!
BUT ZOZIMOS...

GO STAND OVER THERE!
OKAY, GO AHEAD.
CLANG
HEY, COME ON! WHAT IS THIS?

OKAY, FINE!
I GUESS I'M THE BAD GUY, IS THAT IT?!?!
WHERE'S MY STICK!
OH MY, ZOZIMOS, YOU'VE BROKEN IT.
OH, WELL.
I'M JUST GONNA GO BE A HERMIT OR SOMETHING... NOT THAT ANYONE CARES.
WHO'S GOING TO PAY US, THEN?!

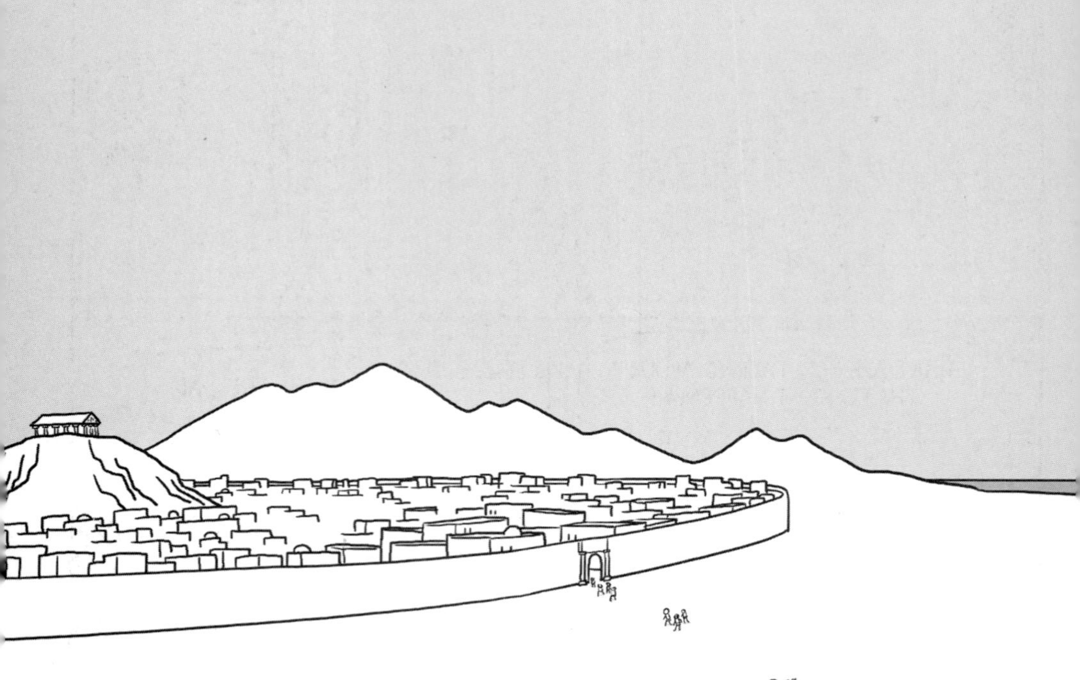

TEN YEARS LATER
...AND SO NESTOR WANDERED OFF, NEVER TO BE SEEN AGAIN...
DAD, THAT'S THE FAKEST STORY I EVER HEARD.
WHAT ARE YOU TALKING ABOUT? THAT'S WHAT HAPPENED!
OH, OKAY, SURE, DAD.
WHAT'S WRONG WITH IT?
TOO MANY EXAGGERATIONS!

PRAXIS KNOCKED OUT A PIECE OF THE SKY?
AND ZEUS HIMSELF CAME DOWN AND TOOK AWAY YOUR GOLDEN FEATHER?
HE DID!
YEAH, HE DID, ACTUALLY.
OR ON NYX'S ISLE, ONE PATH LED TO THE FEATHER AND THE OTHER TO THE LAND OF THE DEAD?
WHAT'S WRONG WITH THAT?
IF IT WAS TRUE, WOULDN'T YOU HAVE GONE BACK THERE AND GOTTEN MOM BACK?

SEE YOU AT DINNER, POPS!
I'M AN IDIOT!
SMACK!

GUYS... GUYS...
PANT PANT
WHAT IS IT?
CATCH YOUR BREATH FIRST!
I HAVEN'T SEEN YOU THIS EXCITED SINCE ZOTIKOS WAS BORN.
ROUND UP THE STICONAUTS! WE'RE GOING ON ANOTHER ADVENTURE!
I THOUGHT YOU WERE DONE WITH THOSE!

THERE'S ALWAYS ANOTHER ADVENTURE!